The Rake's Regression

by

Brent Cheetham

Grosvenor House
Publishing Limited

The right of Brent Cheetham to be identified as the author of this
work has been asserted in accordance with Section 78
of the Copyright, Designs and Patents Act 1988

The book cover picture is copyright to mujdatuzel

This book is published by
Grosvenor House Publishing Ltd
Link House
140 The Broadway, Tolworth, Surrey, Kt6 7Ht.
www.grosvenorhousepublishing.co.uk

A CIP record for this book
is available from the British Library

ISBN 978-1-78623-807-8

PREAMBLE

"A rake, short for rakehell (analogous to hell raiser) is a historic term applied to a man who is habituated to immoral conduct, particularly womanising, often a rake was also prodigal, wasting his (usually inherited) fortune on gambling, wine, woman and song and incurring lavish debts in the process" – *Wikipedia*

What you are (hopefully) about to read needs some explaining. I was a friend of Albert Warren, and used to drink, with him every Thursday night down our local pub for the last hour before closing time. We must have met up almost every Thursday for about ten years. One evening at around closing time, he said to me that I was probably his best friend and the only man he could trust. He said could he drop off a folder at my house at the weekend, and keep it safe for him. I said "sure, no trouble". I did not want to enquire as to the contents of his folder, as he must have had a good logical reason for wanting to deposit it with me. I asked him to come around about 10am next Sunday (could not make Saturday as I was working). He duly turned up at 10am, prompt and to cut a long story short, gave me a folder, and said if he was to die, I was free to have its contents published. Well last month, he was hit by a drunk driver, whist driving home, and died two days later in hospital from his injuries. What follows are the contents of his folder, left to me for safekeeping. Make of it what you will...

Brent Cheetham

PROLOGUE

If there is one thing about us Homo sapiens (which I count myself as a member) it is our inherent ability to use our imagination. This sometimes can be a blessing in disguise. We watch a film or a play and if it's a good one, we suspend reality and forget that the persons we are viewing are only actors, and the backdrops are often only props. Thus it shows us all to be open to manipulation to those who might wish to push us in a direction that is conducive to their own values and needs. This surely has been the fate of mankind since the time of Adam and Eve.

Writers have pushed the notion of utopia and dystopia in equal measure and folks have only been too willing to believe those who propagate these ideas. Maybe the biggest flaw of the human race is our imagination, as we suspend reality in favour of something that gives us comfort and joy – conversely this suspending of reality can take us into a temporary nightmare world as in horror films, which makes us feel all the better and safe when the film concludes. They make us appreciate our own security all the more after the film credits roll. The human race, can produce good men and woman as well as evil men and woman, and it's the bad folk who are often able to realise how susceptible some of us are, and subvert our actions towards the direction of evil without our knowledge. It could well be that our famed human race is nothing but a biological error, that nature in its infinite wisdom will soon rectify.

My uncle Bill (short for William) who passed away in his eighty-eighth year, was according to what I had been informed a bit of a rake in his youth and had been known as a lady's man (a euphemism in his case for being highly promiscuous, despite having a long suffering wife Maud who preceded him, by ten years). He was also, I am reliably informed, involved in a number of 'Sharp' business deals that perhaps were not entirely above board. Uncle Bill had his fingers in too many hot pies, and was deeply entrenched in radical politics throughout his long and eventful life. A life which we could as a family only scratch the surface. He was like an iceberg to us, with ninety per cent hidden under the waterline, and only ten per cent above the sea's surface that we could see. And even that ten per cent was only what he chose to tell us, or somehow things inadvertently disclosed, by way of gossip. I expect most of you readers have had relatives who have been reticent about their lives, and my uncle Bill was no exception.

I had only met Uncle Bill on a few occasions in my youth, but I enjoyed his company and his lively intellect. When he came to Sunday tea there was never a dull moment. But all of a sudden he stopped coming, I was never told why. I understand my father who was twenty years younger than Uncle Bill had some kind of fall out. I must have about aged ten when I last saw Uncle Bill, and my father did not discuss the matter, nor say anything further when I approached him over why we had not seen Uncle Bill of late. He just informed me that I would not be seeing Uncle Bill ever again, and that I was to not ask any questions about it, nor was I allowed to write to him. Since my writing was not up to much at that age, and the fact I did not know his address, only that he lived in a large mansion, somewhere out in the country prohibited me from writing to him. After a few short years the memory of the good times I had with Uncle Bill had been erased from my memory bank, as if he had never placed a foot on our front door mat.

It was with a great surprise that I received a phone call out of the blue from solicitors who asked for Albert Warren. I almost replaced the receiver, after having about a dozen cold callers that day. So I replied in a somewhat surly and disinterested manner, "Why, who wants to know". They replied that they had been instructed by the executors of the will of the late William Warren to trace me, as I had been left "something" in his will. They informed me that they had instigated quite a search to track me down, as there were a number of Mr A. Warrens in the UK. After a prolonged conver-sation in which I seemed to convince them that I indeed was the Mr A. Warren in question they were looking for, I timidly asked them with an air of anticipation what had been left to me. They informed me that they were not at liberty to disclose what had been left to me or discuss the matter further, other than to say that the object would be sent to me once further clarification as to my identity had been received by them. They gave me a list of documents they needed before they could proceed and said they would be in contact again once they confirmed that everything was in order.

I stood in my lounge still holding the phone long after the solicitors; whose name was Peter, Peters & Son had rung off. It was as if the floodgates to my mind had been opened, and all the old memories of Uncle Bill, flooded back in one giant tidal wave. And to be honest with you dear reader, I was intrigued as to what the object was, and to the value of it. If anybody had peeped though the window at that time, I must have looked like Lot's wife turned to a pillar of salt in the Old Testament, I did not move a muscle as I was so deep in thought for what seemed an age. Eventually I snapped out of my self-imposed impression of Nelson's column, and returned to the real world like a parachutist regaining terra firma.

That night I proceeded to collate all the documentation together, and the following morning after photocopying everything, dispatched all that was requested by special delivery. All that was needed of me now was to sit back and wait. One week became two weeks, two weeks became three and three weeks became a month. I did not want to phone or chase up the solicitors as I did not want to be seen as being too pushy and greedy. Eventually after five weeks my long wait that seemed like an eternity came to an end, an end that I did not anticipate. There was a knock on my door, and I opened it to view a smartly dressed man wearing a hat and holding a parcel. He said this is your parcel and that I had to sign for it. I informed him that I had not ordered anything.

He replied, "your name is Albert Warren and you live at twenty-two Station road, am I not correct?"

I said, "yes you are one hundred per cent correct."

"Well this is for you," he replied, "and you will have to sign for it".

I obliged the man by signing and he duly handed me the parcel.

I said, "thank you for this but I have no idea what's in it".

The man smiled and said, "Well hope it's a good surprise for you then". He saluted and said, "have a nice day," as he turned to walk back down the path.

I replied, "and the same to you". I still had not put two and two together and linked this parcel up with Uncle Bill's will, as the only thing I could think of at the time was it was an early birthday present as my birthday was only a week away.

I tore off the brown paper that concealed the parcel, and on opening found a note from Peter, Peters & Son that inform me that the enclosed box had been left to me and they had not opened the box as only Uncle William and I know the code. The code I was informed was the name of the game Uncle Bill used to play with me all those years ago. Yes I remember it well; it was not your normal every day child's game but one Bill had invented himself.

The game my Uncle Bill devised consisted of a kind of 'name that tune', but with a variation. He would hide pennies round the house and garden, and then would whistle a song, which I had to name, and if I got it right and could sing the first line on the song, he would give a clue as to where the penny or pennies were hidden. Like, try the red chair in the lounge, or the small flower-bed to the left of the pond in the back garden. This game he called 'Going for a song'. I tapped in 'Going for a song' on the keyboard on the front of the metal box and pressed the enter button. As soon as I had done this the lid of the box sprung open. I peered into the box, but could find no diamonds, gold or silver or anything of monetary value at all, but just what looked like a leatherbound, diary or book, but with no inscription on the front cover. I opened the book, and the first thing I discovered was a sheet of foolscap paper and handwritten on the top was *'A truncated story of my life'* by William Warren. My first thought was what a let down. However it intrigued me to read on further, perhaps his story would solve the mystery as to why Bill had stopped visiting our house. I would point out at this juncture, that my mother died young, and that my father had suffered a stroke, and was more or less a vegetable and therefore I was never going to get my sole surviving parent to divulge this information.

I read on –

> To my nephew, Albert – well I expect you thought that money or some other items of value would be contained in this box. Don't be aggrieved for what is written on the enclosed pages is worth all the gold buried in Fort Knox. As the old Frank Zappa song goes – 'information is not knowledge, Knowledge is not wisdom, wisdom is not truth, truth is not beauty, beauty is not love, love is not music, music is the best' – The information, knowledge, wisdom and truth (which is always a movable object) contained within these pages, will hopefully be music to your ears. You will not have to suspend reality, for reality is only too real. You were a bright child, and I could see that you want to make sense of the world, as you were always probing me with penetrating questions about the world, showing a marked degree of

an intellect, that few if any folks from older generations would have the questioning mind or even the temerity to ask. It was indeed a pleasure talking to someone like you who reminded me of the young Jesus aged twelve questioning the Elders in the temple of Jerusalem. Although I freely admit I am not a Christian nor hold any brief for any religious group. Indeed I am what was called in bygone days a Rake – a man habituated to immoral conduct. We are what we are and nothing was ever going to change my nature, a lover of fine wine, fine music, fine art and fine woman – last but not least a lover of anybody whose brain cells are capable of rising above the stinking swamp of mankind: Well you said you wanted to understand the world – Now read on!

What was contained within the books pages was indeed a revelation. What follows is not a verbatim transcript of my uncle's book, as I have taken the liberty of deleting trivial and sometimes rambling sections and passages from his manuscript, as I see no reason why I should bore the reader more than necessary.

Part One

BILL WARREN'S STORY
(AND CONFESSION)

As a young man I saw the world as my oyster. I viewed the world and its social institutions with the air of a cynic. I came to an early inescapable conclusion, that it was a dog eat dog world, in which only scum rises to the surface. I viewed the great and the good with a degree of envy and yes I have to admit admiration. Some folk had reached the higher echelons of society, by dint of their sheer hard work. Hard work brought me out in the shivers, and I thought to myself, that there must be a way of reaching the pinnacle of society without working my nose to the grindstone. Even at school I looked at my fellow school chums as being fools. They appeared to me nothing but sheep, as they followed, their heroes like football stars, and football teams. Others followed religion blindly, or gave unequivocal support to political parties. I could see how easy it was to lead them and misdirect theses idiots on any path chosen by their heroes. When they spoke of their chosen subject, they claimed to be clever and spoke original thoughts, when in fact they were little more than Poll Parrots repeating things unconsciously fed into their tiny heads from above.

However I kept all this to myself, and I remained a popular chap with my fellow schoolmates, who through my wit and dare I say charm, kept the boys on my side whilst I used my charm to captivate the girls, which often brought physical results, which were to my liking. Basically I was a hedonistic fraud, who could almost get everybody dancing to my fiddle. I was not a 'Hard nut' as I never used violence, or the threat of violence to achieve my goals. That I left to the numbskulls, which used brawn over brain. Those who used brawn over brain were constantly been caught out and in trouble with the school authorities. For many of them this characteristic habit was retained in later life, only this time the head-master's office was replicated by the courtrooms.

I sure could use my time more constructively, as they fought to gain the mere material detritus of society. They were out to catch minnows, whilst I was out to catch sharks. And so it was I decided to go into business as they say. Business to my mind is more often than not, little more than the art of deception, as we use sleight of hand to create in the minds of the gullible, needless wants. Thus I became a past master in the dark arts of deception and illusion. I never got caught out, as my moto was always keep the client happy and contented whenever you can, as that way, they hardly ever complain. It's also a human failing, that proud folk (which was my specialty in dealing with), would be the last to kick up a ruck, if they think they have been deceived. Hence they tend to go numb, rather than shout to the world, that such clever folks as them had been led up the garden path.

But all this material wealth was not enough, I wanted status and adoration. In the 1960s and 1970s one way to get noticed was to go into politics. Politics is a silly game, which can reap great rewards to those who know the rules, and know how to play the game. But me being me, I did not look to the establishment parties for advancement but to radical politics. So I joined the Radical party, which could use my unique talents as a speaker who could cajole its members to do almost anything I wanted. There is one thing about all political parties; most of the rank and file have blind faith in the cause. Blind faith is conducive to anybody who wants to sell them anything. In my case I was not selling goods and chattels, but an idealistic dream of utopia. To me utopia is like a bubble, you just try to catch it in your hands and it bursts. Bubbles like utopia are but a fleeting apparition, which only the plebeians believe in.

Being a speaker I always had to over simplify things and I railed against religion by proclaiming that all religious establishments are wrong and evil, and that all their adherents, were either evil or fools. Likewise I said only atheists or agnostics can only do no harm on earth. In the real world, being atheists does not automatically make you a good person; any more than being a Christian makes you a good person. We all have faults, as we are all too human. I ridiculed the secularists as being weak on religion and called for all places of worship, to be torn down, and religion banned. I said we don't need a secular society, where religious rights are protected, and the state and religion are made separate. Religion should be outlawed as it pollutes mankind. I found a receptive audience for my flawed rhetoric. But this was the 1960s and 1970s where almost anything goes. Britain had lost its

empire and folks were looking at something to believe in.
I was there to take advantage of the vacuum, thus created.

My background was hardly one of poverty, and yet I
was seen as the champion of the working man or
woman. I paid lip service to feminism, and yet was a
misogynist myself. I married young, and soon found,
out that my wife Maud, was unable to have children,
and so the prospect of a happy married normal life, as
seen by many at that time, was never going to happen. I
lived in a large house (some would say mansion) in the
Hertfordshire countryside. The family's money I was
told came from the slave trade and I understand from
my father that his great, great, great grandfather was a
cunning and ruthless man. In mitigation for my family's
actions in the past, I always said we were in tune with
the times, and quoted the fact that even the Church of
England was involved with the Slave trade (or Africa
trade as it was sometimes called). I cited the fact that
one of the churches best known hymns *'Amazing Grace'*
was composed by the slave trader and clergyman John
Newton (1725–1807) published in 1779, and that John
Newton did not become an abolitionist until 1788.
Most folk seemed happy with my weak defence of my
family's past nefarious actions.

I gambled heavily on stocks and shares, which to me
was more fun than frequenting any casino. I started up a
number of companies, whose actives were barely the
right side of the law. I was often juggling money around
from one company to the next in order to avoid credi-
tors or the tax man. I understood the argot of the business world and folks would say to me that I had the 'gift
of the gab'. I was living life in the fast lane and enjoying
every minute of it. However my debts began to mount

and my love life was a mess. Maud bless her cotton socks, must have known or suspected what I was up to, but she never let on or say a word as I was the man of the house, who paid all the bills. But all this was about to change.

First of all I must apologize to the reader, as it was many years ago, when my political standing was at its height, so some of the facts are little more than a blur. l was standing by the wall, in some county village hall, which had been booked by the young radicals for an after meeting disco. I remember distinctly feeling as pleased as punch, as my latest speech had gone down well to rapturous applause. I remember there being an old black stand up piano in the corner, and that the floor under my feet, had some kind of brown stain on it. Funny the silly things you remember when you get old. ln those days I always went out alone leaving Maud at home, which left me with a free hand to do my own thing. I remember eyeing up the local talent, thinking there was some good looking crumpet, on the dance floor. I never got 'cup shot' at these do's, as no young floozy is ever impressed by a drunken suitor.

I swear to god I had only drunk no more than one gin and lime, and in no way could I be described cup shot or inebriated. And yet all of a sudden I felt faint and a tad dizzy, the room and the floor with its brown stain mark began to move back and forth. I was beginning to get the distinct impression that the old black upright piano was sliding towards me. I tried to focus on a good looking young lady on the dance floor but to no avail, the room kept spinning round and round, as if there was an earth-quake or earth tremor. The one thing my still functioning brain could make out was that nobody else was affected by this earth tremor and I deduced from that, it was me having the problem and not the environment itself.

So without letting on that perhaps I was ill, I made my apologies, to the small group of folks I was talking to me by saying, "excuse me ladies and gents, l just wish to pop out to get a breath of fresh air". I remember trying to walk straight and I heard in the background a male voice saying, "it looks like he has had, one over the eight". I walked out of the main hall, down a short corridor, past the gents and ladies toilets. This was executed not without difficulty as on at least two occasions I had to use my hands against the wall as a prop. The last thing I remember was standing in the car park, taking in the cold fresh night air and staring up to the twinkling stars, on a cloudless night. That's all I can remember about that night, as after that everything went blank'

Part Two

INTO THE ABYSS

I awoke to find myself sitting rather uncomfortably on what could only be described as an old fashioned child's wooden school chair. I had my hands spread out on either side of a Victorian children's school desk, complete with an ink well in the top right hand corner, with the customary ink stain extending out from the centre of the ink pot. l tried to move my hands, but found that they were transfixed to the top of the table. All around was a dark blur and the first thought that entered my mind was that perhaps some opponent had slipped something into my drink, maybe some kind of drug or a Mickey Finn. Then I thought crossed my mind I must be in a dream. So I looked down at my hands, and observed the small birth mark on my left hand, which confirmed to me, that this was no dream but real life. Slowly but surely my eyesight started to come back and adjust to my surroundings. The place was chilly but not cold, and at this stage I had no idea if the place l was in was as big as the airship hangers at Cardington or in a small boxroom. Next I tried to speak by saying is there anybody there, but although I could say the words in my mind, nothing emanated from my mouth. I was as helpless as a new born baby. I just sat there as if in a trance unable to move my feet, my arms or move a muscle, as if I was shackled to the chair in fetters, and unable to do or say anything.

The monotony was eventually broken as a small light was turned on; it was a light bulb, hanging from a length of wire in front of me bereft of any light shade. I just viewed this naked bulb and cable hanging from the ceiling and contemplated, that if the people who put me here used a cable, this place was unlikely to be an airship hanger, aircraft hangar or a warehouse, as the ceiling must not be too far above me. After a while I could make out, that there was a rather large corpulent man standing behind the bright shining light. I could just make out through the diffused light that he was aged about sixty and he sported a neat trimmed beard. At long last the figure spoke, "I am glad you could make it here for a nice friendly chat," said the bulk.

The Bulk continued, "I see you are coming round, just to explain to you, you will not have the use of your limbs, for some time, nor have the ability to speak. So until your speech returns, which should not be long now, you will have to communicate by way of eye movement. One blink should indicate the affirmative or yes and two blinks should represent the negative or no. So to kick off Mr Warren, can you hear me and do you understand the gist of what I am saying?"

I felt I had no option but to go along with the bulks game, after all what were the alternatives. So a responded by giving my left eye a slow, deliberate wink.

"Splendid, splendid," said the bulk, "no harm done, nothing ventured, nothing gained.

"Just to point out," said the bulk, "as you regain the use of your limbs, it would be unwise to try and leave us without permission."

At this I observed two beefy sentinels step forward, from the darkness behind the bulk to stand erect either side of him. Both appeared to be carrying some large weapon, but I could not make out what the weapon was, a machine gun, a sword, a sabre, or some kind of large club?

The bulk gave it a few seconds for it to sink in and then went on to say: "We have been watching you with a considerable degree of interest, you appear to be a smart and intelligent person, would that be fair to say Mr Warren?"

I gave one blink to indicate the affirmative in reply.

"We are a good judge of character, and believe that you, like us, believe that a stable society, is conducive to the wellbeing and happiness of all its citizens, however you being a leading speaker for the radical party has raised a few eyebrows in certain quarters, Now I am sure you can blind your followers with your eloquent, but meaningless, flapdoodle and codswallop, and whilst we accept you are nothing more than a rake and a mountebank, we do strongly believe that you can be of use to us and your country. You see Mr Warren we know all about your sexual peccadillos and your shady, and may I be bold enough to say criminal business deals.

"You are little more a snake oil salesman," the bulk went on. "Your gambling on high risk ventures on the stock market portrays another one of your weakness – Greed. Our information leads us to conclude that you have a mountain of debt, which could bring the whole house of Warren into a state of collapse. Am I not correct Mr Warren?"

l tried to speak but all that came out was "Ah".

The bulk said – "Oh good, you appear to be getting your voice back Mr Warren, will not be long now before your vocal cords are back in full working order – ln the meantime was that 'Ah' a yes or a no?"

I blinked once for a yes.

The bulk went on as if he was a schoolteacher, speaking to a nine-year-old child with an exceedingly patronising tone of voice, "l should not be having to tell you this, but the only true folk who appreciate the law and support the law of this land are not the common folk, but the criminal fraternity. Not your petty criminal mind you, who still thinks all coppers are bastards, but the true criminal like you – who needs the state to protect any ill-gotten gains. Your lifestyle depends on the police doing their job, can't have any petty criminals upsetting your apple cart, and attacking you or stealing from you can we?"

By this time I was regaining my voice and replied with a faint, "yes, I take your point".

"Yes," he went on, "your average professional criminal, your bent banker, your insider trader, your dodgy politician, even your most outrageous money grabbing religious leader, loves the police. The police are their security blanket, they may try and hide things from the police and the state, but they need the police like a bird needs its wings. Can you see what I am driving at Mr Warren?"

I replied with a faint "yes" to the bulk.

"We as a precaution have placed at least one of our operatives in each and every radical political group that has been brought to our attention in the country. Most, "the bulk went on, "are there to observe but some are placed as agent provocateurs – But we have to be discreet about matters, and we do not even inform our operatives who the other operatives are. Some of the radical groups we have set up ourselves as honey traps and we have a high rate of success in this regard". The bulk gave a wry smile, "in fact it amuses me to think that in one radical group every one of their inner circle is one of our operatives, and none of them are any the wiser. Sorry Mr Warren I have digressed – As no doubt you can appreciate we cannot foresee every eventuality and it goes without saying that every now and again groups spring up which are not under our ultimate control – it's a hard job we do and it's never ending, like painting the Forth Bridge. Now back to you Mr Warren we would like you willing to help us?"

I took my time trying to formulate my reply, was I to appear angry, or frustrated, or shall I appear, calm, cool and collected. I opted for a more aggressive approach and replied, "What choice do I have? If I refused to work for you; no doubt I would find myself in the gutter decapitated some dark and windy night".

"Come, come Mr Warren what do you think we all are, jungle savages? We are all civilised people here, we would not dream of such a thing, we are a civil organization whose only job is to help mankind and relive suffering in the world".

"So what happens if I refuse your kind offer?" I retorted.

"Why nothing whatsoever," said the bulk – other than your story of your little infidelities will be leaked to the national press and I am not sure what that will do for your squeaky clean image, and in addition you will find yourself in court over your various nefarious business activities, which I am also certain you will find yourself as a result of the court proceedings financially impecunious".

By this time I had regained control of my limbs and I banged my fist on the table shouting, "Why that's blackmail – I don't call that very civilised".

"Now calm yourself down Mr Warren, take a deep breath and count to ten." He waited whilst I calmed down and my blood pressure was back to normal. "Now that's better Mr Warren can't have you stimulating a cardiac arrest. Just for the record we don't use the word blackmail here, we call it our little incentives. Is that clear Mr Warren?"

"Well how are you going to get the press to not report about me, if I turn down your little incentives? Don't tell me you control the press."

"No one controls the press, but we do have a number of reporters at our beck and call, who would be obliged to do a nice piece on you."

"No doubt," I said, "only after you blackmailed, sorry I mean gave them little incentives".

"Now, now Mr Warren we are only trying to do you a favour, by keeping your name out of the paper, and you reply in a most discourteous way."

"Well what is in it for me, what kind of remuneration are you going to offer me?"

"Why nothing," he replied, "is not keeping your name out of the paper and saving you from bankruptcy enough?"

Just how do you propose to save me from bankruptcy I replied?"

"All in good time, all in good time," replied the bulk, "first of all let me explain what your unpaid job will entail. We have two types of operatives, you will be just a category B operative, all you have to do is report back to us about anybody who proposes to undertake any illegal activities and before you ask, a category A operative has been trained by us from the very start and is a full-time operative who receives a stipend for his or her valuable work. As you can see the work is not too sedulous and I feel it will be just up your street. So what do you say Mr Warren a yay or a nay?"

"Well you don't seem to give me much choice," I replied.

"That's the spirit we like to hear," the bulk went on. "There is an old military saying – time spent on reconnaissance is rarely wasted – and that is in a nutshell what we do, and you will play a small but invaluable role for us, and your country."

I interjected by saying, "you said you were going to sort out my financial problems once I had agreed to work for you, so how do you propose to do that?"

"Ah Mr Warren, I wondered when you would come back to that subject. We will not be giving you cash, if that's what you mean. What we propose to do is have one of our front companies offer a grossly inflated figure for one of your ailing companies, with this you should be able to pay off any debt's, and put you on a firm financial footing. And a word or warning Mr Warren we are not authorised to give you any further financial help. We are not a charity."

"So you can guarantee that my name will not get in the press then?" I said to the bulk.

"No guarantee whatsoever," replied the Bulk. "All we can do, is not release the current information we have on you to the press. So my advice to you is to be very careful about any future assignations, better still cut them out altogether. If a reporter or the press gets hold of the 'dirt' on you independently from us there is nothing we can do to stop them going to print. Likewise keep your business clean and above board as we are unable to bail you out, for any future financial improprieties. Do you understand Mr Warren?"

"I think you have made that abundantly clear," I replied.

"How will I contact you in the future," I asked the bulk?

"It's not a case of you contacting us, it's more of a case of us contacting you if we need you to verify something or need information. However on rare occasions we will expect you to contact us – You will be given the details of an obscure gardening magazine which operates via a PO box number and a telephone number of the editor, you should not phone unless it's an emergency otherwise you can post any information we require to the PO box number."

"It seems you have all got this well worked out," I said to the bulk, "all very professional."

"Well we like to think so," replied the Bulk.

Next thing I recall everything went as quiet as a morgue. The bulk appeared to disappear from view, and I got that distinctly dizzy feeling again. I went into a semi catatonic state and became unconscious.

Part Three

BACK TO THE REAL WORLD!

Next thing I recall was a fuzzy face looking down at me, and then I heard a male voice saying, "I think he is coming round now," and just as before things slowly came back into focus. I awoke to find a nurse and a female doctor beside the bed I was lying in.

"Good afternoon," said the female doctor, "welcome back to the land of the living Mr Warren."

"Where am I?" l asked inquisitively.

"In hospital, you were found lying in a ditch not two hours ago suffering from acute influenza, luckily for you a passer-by found you, as you could have died from hypothermia from lying in that damp soggy ditch – consider yourself a lucky man to be alive. Just take some rest now and you will soon be as fit as a fiddle."

"Hold on," I said (my mind was still not fully awake). "How do you know my name is Warren?"

"We found your wallet, and all your details are in there."

"Oh," I replied, "that's obvious, sorry I have not got my brain back to full working order yet."

"That's understandably," replied the doctor, "now get some rest."

The female doctor continued, "we have taken the liberty of contacting your wife and she will be along to collect you as soon as we feel you are fit to go home, and in the meantime we are just going to give you a sedative."

The sedative was administered and I slept like a log for hours. When I woke up, I was given my clothes and was told that my wife was outside waiting for me. I slipped my clothes back on and went to meet my wife after saying thank you to the hospital staff. My wife did not say much (She never did) other to say, "I am told it's safe to take you home now," and that the doctor said she should drive me home as I may not be safe to drive yet. The hospital gave me some tablets to take and we walked to the car park, found the car and drove off. As we were driving back, a thought crossed my mind – better check my wallet, as I had a small sum of cash in it. I opened my wallet, and counted the cash, and it was all there to the last pound. Then a noticed a card in my wallet, l pulled it out as l did not recognise it – it was a card for a gardening magazine, with a PO box number and a phone number on.

They say it takes a long spoon to sup with the devil – But I was not sure who the devil really is, could it be the radical party I had joined, or the group in which I was to become one of their operatives. Or maybe it's me, perhaps I am the devil and I don't know it? And the organization, was I right to assume it was the British secret service at work? After a while I dismissed the idea that they could be anybody else. Then the thought flashed into my mind, maybe I should go to the press about it and expose the workings of the British government. But would they believe me and print the story? I very much doubt it and what if they did print the story, would I not just look a fool and a crackpot? I had visions of been carried away in a straightjacket to Colney Hatch. And if I thought that, then the organization knows I will be thinking that, therefore it did not appear to me to be a viable option. My next thought was to take a lower profile within the radical party, that way perhaps the organization will take less interest with me and leave me alone altogether.

Two or three weeks passed without any contact with the organization. Then one day I got into a lift at a hotel I was staying in and as I was about to close the door a skinny looking man with a bowler hat, briefcase and umbrella jumped in at the last moment. The man look like the very antithesis of the fat man who had inter-viewed me, he looked strange as even then the bowler hat was going out of fashion.

"Sublime to the ridiculous," l said to myself. Then without warning the lift stopped between floors. The skinny man turned to me and said, "we are a tad disap-pointed with you – you appear to have not contacted us as requested."

"l was about to reply when the skinny chap said that's not too much of a problem as it appears there is not a great deal to report. lts your last two speeches. They appear to have lost their vim, vigour and vitality. What happened to your demands that we do away with the royal family, the landed gentry and the banking class? Now I do hope you are not trying to be clever, as you know what to expect if you become too clever, we expect a marked improvement in your performance." At the end of the sentence the lift started working again, and the skinny man got off on the next floor without me uttering a single word

Well the next speech I gave was a right over the top belter; I called for the royal family, the landed gentry and the banking class to be hung from street lampposts, as that is what they deserve. The audience went wild. Two days later I received an offer to buy one of my companies at a price I could not refuse to turn down. I had been caught hook, line and sinker, no turning back now.

So for the rest of my working days and beyond I was leading a double life. However the work was not too arduous, just passing on snippets of information to my unseen controllers. I hope this information has been of help to you Albert, as I am not the working class hero that I have been made out to be. The world is not as simple as some folks make out and no individual should be any body's hero. Paying homage to anybody shows you are a sheep, and not a lion. No book has ever contained all the truth, and the old saying doing things by the book, means you lack imagination and are unable to think for yourself. When you hear politicians talk, it's best to remain cynical. There is an old Latin saying 'Cui Bono' or who stands to benefit, so that when unexplained things happen in this world it's always best to ask who stands to profit by them? Beware of folks in authority, as it's all too easy to lead folks down the garden path like pigs to the slaughter.

Yours William (Bill) Warren.

Part Four

ALBERT WARREN
CONTINUES THE STORY

I read Bills story cover to cover, and it still did not give a clue as to why he stopped visiting us all those years ago. As for the story itself, no dates given, no names, no places, very little I could check up on to confirm. Indeed there was nothing to confirm when he had written the manuscript. I made further enquiries about Uncle Bill and found out that he spent the last eight years of his life in a sanatorium and further enquires with them disclosed that he was unable to write a cheque when he was deposited with them, let alone write a manuscript.

On double checking with the solicitors, they also confirmed that his will and testament (with the box) was deposited five years before he was admitted into the sanatorium. So could his comments about his life be true, or were they a figment of his imagination. Maybe he was going a bit gaga five years before his long-term stay in the mental hospital? Indeed there was no radical party as such, at the time Uncle Bill was said to operate; however there were several parties and groups around at that time calling themselves radical, and indeed further investigation confirmed that Bill had been involved with some of these. I continued to search out some of his old colleagues and ask questions, (although I did not reveal why I was asking, nor the contents of his manuscript) all this appeared to be of to no avail, and I kept coming up against a blank wall. But I was not prepared to give up my search for the truth.

Then one day whilst walking home from the pub, a car screeched to a stop besides me and two burly men bundled me into the rear of the car. They said nothing and drove a couple of miles out of our village. They stopped by a layby in the local woods, and the man in the front left hand seat turned around and said, "I understand you have been asking questions about the late Mr William Warren – and I have a little friendly advice for you, if you care about your physical health and wellbeing I strongly advise that you desist in asking questions about your uncle Bill."

What choice did I have, other than to agree with them? They then drove me back almost home the guy in the front said thanks for my understanding and shook my hand. Whatever Bill was up to it was clearly unsavoury. Did Uncle gave me the whole truth and nothing but the truth? Who knows? But as Bill himself says nobody should have heroes, and we should all be cynical about what politicians say, as after all is said the done Uncle Bill was a politician first and foremost.

Lightning Source UK Ltd.
Milton Keynes UK
UKHW010849310123
416239UK00001B/155